Fro

Th

of Halloween!

Love, Nana + Bumpa
October, 2017

James Sutherland

CONTENTS

Rhubarb or Bust.

Frogarty Spittleflap was a witch and an ugly one at that. Many people believe that beauty is only skin deep and that it is our personalities, our *inner* beauty that really matters; although this may often be true, it is irrelevant in this instance because Frogarty was *just* as horrid on the inside as she was on the outside.

Short and squat in stature, her features were gruesome to the extent that a single glance in her direction was often enough to make a strong man physically sick. We must not pity her though, reader, because Frogarty was also mean. She was so mean that even her pet cat, Scratch, despised her and only hung around their little cottage in the woods in the hope of scrounging a few leftovers from one of Frogarty's foul meals. Have we talked about Frogarty's diet yet? Perhaps it's better if we don't – it could be that you've just had your supper and might begin to feel a little queasy if we were to go into too much detail... Are you *sure*? Ok – if you insist...

Well, reader, Frogarty did not eat the kinds of things that you or I might enjoy. She had probably never even *heard* of sausages or spaghetti bolognese or fish and chips or chicken nuggets – she only ate *horrible* things. To give you an idea what is meant by 'horrible things' just have a look at the menu that she drew up for the day on which our story begins…

Starters:

Live maggots with a rich, creamy woodlouse sauce.

Rotten owl's egg, nestling on a bed of bogies.

Caterpillar soup, with a hint of toenail.

Mains:

Braised slugs with toadstool mash.

Pan fried squirrel, marinated in armpit sweat.

Badger Burger with earwax relish.

Dessert:

Fly pie with toad slime custard.

Jellied earwigs.

Rhubarb crumble.

"*Rhubarb crumble?*" I hear you cry. "But *surely* there's nothing horrible about that?"

I'm afraid there is, reader. You see, when normal people make rhubarb crumble, they do so using the rhubarb *stalks*, which are very tasty indeed. Frogarty, on the other hand always throws the stalks away, preferring to make *her* rhubarb crumble using only the *leaves*, which are poisonous. So there you have it – there is *nothing whatsoever* on Frogarty's menu that would be considered fit for human consumption.

Having polished off the last few forkfuls of braised slugs, Frogarty leaned back in her rickety rocking chair to consider her choice of desert. Fly pie had given her terrible wind last time she had eaten it and she'd already had jellied earwigs twice this week. All things considered, there was but one option available: rhubarb crumble.

"Hmmmmmm," she slavered, licking her grey, shrivelled lips with anticipation as she shuffled through to her larder. "I *love* rhubarb crumble, me!" But when she looked in the box where the rhubarb leaves were kept, it was empty!

"Gaaaaaaaargh!" she shrieked in dismay. "*Who's pinched me rhubarb?*"

Because he was the only other inhabitant of the cottage, Frogarty had a habit of blaming Scratch, her cat, whenever anything went missing. *Where was that meddlesome moggy?* Fortunately for him, Scratch was nowhere to be seen.

"I shall have me rhubarb if it's the last thing I do!" Frogarty cried as she bustled through to the living room to obtain her book of spells. Grasping

the ancient volume, she plonked her fat bottom down on the rocking chair and studied the index.

"Aha!" she exclaimed. "Here we go – *Instant Rhubarb*. Page nine hundred and seventy-three." Drooling, she hurriedly turned to the correct page and began to read.

To make instant rhubarb, first take the tongues of three camels... Frogarty stopped. Frogarty frowned. She did not have the tongues of three camels, having used up the last of her supply last Tuesday. There was no alternative; if she wanted rhubarb, she would have to *buy* some, just like any normal person.

"Grrrrr," she grumbled. "I shall have to go to the supermarket. I *hate* going to the supermarket."

Her hideous features twisted with irritation, she reached for her pointy hat and stomped out through the front door of the cottage, slamming it behind her. As she trudged through the woods, animals, birds and even insects fled in terror in all directions. They knew the horrid old hag and understood all too well how mean she could be; if one did not wish to end up as an ingredient in one of her spells, it was wise to avoid contact with Frogarty at all costs.

Arriving at the edge of town, she paused and scratched the huge wart on the end of her chin. It was a bright and sunny day. Frogarty *hated* bright and sunny days. From her position behind a bush she shuddered as she studied the supermarket's window panes glinting in the sun. Frogarty *hated* supermarkets even more than she hated bright and sunny days. Her one consolation was that the rhubarb would be situated in the fruit and vegetable section of the store, and that this was located very close to the front doors. *At least she wouldn't have to venture very far into the awful place; no – she would be back in her cottage, deep in the nice, dark woods in no time, enjoying a huge bowl of rhubarb crumble...*

Frogarty was about to leave her hiding place when she hesitated. The sight of the supermarket had reminded her of her last visit many years beforehand. It had been a total disaster and had ended with several innocent shoppers being admitted to hospital. Though unconcerned about their fate, Frogarty had *not* enjoyed the resulting pursuit through the woods by the police. *No – this time, she did not want there to be any fuss and the only way to achieve this would be for her to enter the supermarket in disguise*. Though she had left her book of spells back at the cottage, she was fairly confident that she could remember one which would conceal her identity. Some kind of magic hat would suffice, provided it could be pulled down over her eyes to hide most of her face.

"Shalacomooga! Zanzibambam!" she croaked. There was a flash, followed by a fizzing sound and a puff of purple smoke. Frogarty could not see herself, however, she was conscious of an

increased weight on her head, as though her witch's hat had been replaced by something noticeably heavier.

"Humff!" she groaned as she groped at the new headgear with her knobbly fingers. *A Mexican sombrero! She could have sworn that Shalacomooga Zanzibambam was the spell for a baseball cap! Never mind – it would have to do. She would only be in the supermarket for a minute anyway...*

To begin with, surprisingly few people at the Costalot Superstore in Lower Bottomton paid any attention to the small, waddling figure in a sombrero as it passed through the automatic doors and headed past the cigarette counter towards the fruit and vegetable isle. Everyone was too busy trying to steer their trolleys or control their children as they sought out the best deals of the day. Indeed, it was only when Frogarty reached the checkout, basket of rhubarb in hand, that the trouble started.

"Would you like any help with your packing?" the pimply youth on the till grunted robotically. His name was Ryan. It said so on his little badge. Having delivered his opening gambit, he glanced up at the customer and smiled, this being precisely what he had been instructed to do whilst training for the role. Unfortunately, Frogarty, who had up to now managed to keep her features hidden beneath the wide brim of her sombrero, looked up at the very same moment in order to respond to the question.

"No I don't!" she barked, looking the hapless checkout operator straight in the eye. "Can't you see? I've only got me rhubarb!"

Although the sombrero still partially shielded the poor fellow from the full impact of Frogarty's face, he had nevertheless, in that fleeting moment, seen more than enough.

"W... Wh... Whaaa..." he croaked, the colour draining from his spotty visage.

"I said that I don't need any help with me packing, 'cos I've only got me *RHUBARB!*" Frogarty roared.

His mouth opening and closing like a goldfish, Ryan groped for the buzzer that he used when he needed assistance from his supervisor. Within seconds, a tubby little woman with an officious air came bustling forth, sweating profusely from the rigours of the job. Her name was Brenda - It said as much on her supervisor's badge which, though more impressive than Ryan's, constituted little more than a speck on her enormous bosom.

"Can I help?" she asked. Unable to elicit a response from the unfortunate lad who was still trembling behind his till, Brenda turned to examine the troublesome customer. Examining Frogarty is invariably a mistake and should never be attempted under any circumstances. So great was her horror, that the burly supervisor fainted into a rack of chewing gum and travel mints, sending the whole display crashing to the floor. The sudden commotion produced a startled squeal from another lady further back in the queue and Frogarty, curious to know what all the fuss was about, turned her face towards her. The sight of the witch's gruesome visage was enough to send the poor woman reeling backwards into her trolley; this, in turn, rammed the knees of a small child sitting in a pushchair. Outraged at this unprovoked assault upon his person, the child responded with an ear-splitting scream.

It was becoming apparent to Frogarty that things were not going quite according to plan, and it occurred to her that it was high time she fled the scene; already, she had observed a balding, overweight security guard striding purposefully towards the growing hubbub. Still clutching her basket of rhubarb, she proceeded hastily towards the exit.

"Hey!" the security guard bellowed. "You just stop there a minute!" His name, incidentally, was Geoff, though he did not have a little badge to advertise the fact.

But Frogarty was not stopping for anybody. She passed through the first set of automatic doors and was surging through the foyer when disaster struck; Geoff the security guard, now in hot pursuit, had pressed the emergency red button that closed the main exit!

“Gaaaaargh!” Frogarty shrieked as she saw the huge metal doors closing ahead of her. It was only the brim of her sombrero that saved her, as it prevented the doors from shutting for a vital split second whilst the rest of her passed through unscathed.

“Hee hee!” she cackled. Her exhilaration was, however, short-lived; although she had managed to squeeze her fat belly through the closing doors in the nick of time, the sombrero had been crushed beyond repair! Frogarty had been growing rather fond of her sombrero... Worse still, in her frantic bid for freedom, the horrid old hag had been forced to abandon her beloved basket of rhubarb! From the relative safety of the car park, she could only watch in frustration as Geoff examined it, his chubby face a picture of bewilderment. In his twenty-seven years as a security guard, he had never known of anyone attempting to steal rhubarb before...

*

In the safety of Spittleflap Cottage, Frogarty nestled into her creaky rocking chair and turned to her spell book. It was an extremely hefty volume; in addition to a myriad of spells, it also contained brief notes about the individual ingredients, together with clear instructions as to how and where they might be obtained.

"Tumty-tumty tum," she hummed as she flicked through the huge, dusty volume. Frogarty had a *terrible* singing voice; even Scratch the cat, whose eerie wailings were the torment of every creature in the forest when he was turfed out into the cold each night, would easily have beaten Frogarty had they ever appeared on X-Factor.

"Let me see... Ah yes – here we are!" she croaked. "I shall have me rhubarb in no time." Drooling with anticipation, she scanned the relevant entry which read as follows:

Rhubarb. Leafy plant. Member of the dock family with edible leaves, though the stalks are toxic. Commonly found in Russia along the banks of the Volga River and in parts of China.

"Russia!" Frogarty shrieked, springing from her rocking chair in dismay. "*China!* I shall never get me rhubarb at this rate! *Scratch! – Fetch me broom!* I'm just nipping to Russia but I'll be back in time for tea."

In reply, Scratch merely rattled his empty dish suggestively with his paw. *Back in time for tea?* he pondered miserably *I haven't even had my lunch yet!*

But Frogarty was in no mood to sympathise with her malnourished moggy. She was on a mission: She would have rhubarb crumble for tea if it killed her. And that, reader, is what it *almost* did...

Hurtling through the sky on her broomstick, Frogarty soon found herself high up above the clouds. With her lank, grey hair fluttering behind her in the wind, she continued to soar upwards until she reached a height where she was *almost* in outer space. At last year's Witches Convention, it had been strongly recommended that any long-distance travel should be undertaken at this height as the lower atmosphere contained too many skyscrapers, aeroplanes, helicopters and other potentially dangerous obstacles.

"Now then... Where's me rhubarb?" she muttered as she squinted down at the spinning blue and green planet far below. For thousands of years, the witches of the world had used the position of the moon and stars to find their way around the skies. Peering out at the Galaxy, its glittering constellations stretching endlessly before her, Frogarty frowned. The moon, she was ok with... Yes – she was *pretty sure* it was that big, round lump of grey rock just over there. Equally, she was fairly confident as the whereabouts of the sun... Yes – it was *definitely* that massive, hot, orangey-coloured thing a bit further away that was making her armpits all sweaty... But beyond this, Frogarty's knowledge of the cosmos was sketchy to say the least. *If only she had paid more attention at school, instead of spending all her time drawing rude pictures of her teacher on the back of her exercise book...* It was with a vague sense of guilt that she reached out her bony hand and, after a brief fumble around the front of her broomstick, switched on the sat-nav.

Although satellite navigation can be a useful thing, in this instance, it proved to be Frogarty's undoing. You see, reader, in order for satellite navigation to work, there has to be satellites circling the earth. They are not in outer space, nor are they in what we call 'the sky', but somewhere in between, a place that is sometimes referred to as 'orbit', which is precisely where Frogarty happened to be at this particular moment in time. When the Witch Queen had ordered her minions to fly at this height to avoid aircraft, she had failed to take into account the huge numbers of satellites flitting about the place. Frogarty had barely typed the first three letters of the word "Russia," into her sat-nav machine, when she was struck forcibly by one of said objects.

"Eek!" she yelped as her broomstick lurched into a brief tailspin before commencing its long, terrifying descent towards the planet below.

*

Most of our larger towns and cities have what is called a *sewage works* situated somewhere nearby. Whenever we flush a toilet, its contents are sent into the sewers, long pipes which run below the ground, which take all the nasty stuff to the sewage works where it can be dealt with accordingly.

At the Lower Bottomton plant, Nigel Fetorworth, recent winner of the Lower Bottomton Sewage Company's *Employee of the Month* award, had enjoyed a deeply satisfying morning. There was something hypnotic about the sight of the enormous vats of raw, untreated waste, bubbling away as it was stirred by the huge, mechanised whisks, which spoke to the very depths of his soul. Indeed, the only thing troubling him was that it was now getting quite late into the afternoon and he would soon be forced to leave his beloved sewage and return home to his wife, Stacey. Nigel was not fond of his wife, nor was she fond of him. As a young girl growing up, Stacey had always dreamed of marrying a Premier League footballer. When, a few days after the wedding, Nigel had announced his decision to pursue a career at the sewage works, it had thus come as a great disappointment to her, a feeling that even her husband's recent triumph at the *Employee of the Month* awards had done little to dispel.

"She's not the woman I married... She'll *never* understand the joys of sewage," poor Nigel sighed as he prepared to clock off for the day. But as he began to descend the wrought iron steps that led down to the office, he heard a curious sound. It began as a high-pitched whistling noise and it came from somewhere high up in the atmosphere.

Shielding his eyes from the early evening sun, Nigel squinted towards the heavens. Bit by bit, the whistling grew louder until he was finally able to detect a small, round speck descending rapidly towards him.

"Crikey!" he gibbered. "It's a meteorite!" For a few seconds, he goggled at the hurtling object, tracing its downward trajectory. "*No!*" he cried when the realisation struck him. "*It's going to land in me sewage!*" Accepting that there was nothing he could do to avert disaster, Nigel turned and fled for his life.

When he breathlessly reported the incident to his boss a few moments later, he was taken aback by his superior's incredulous response.

"But Mr Hodgson, it's *true!*" Nigel whimpered. "There *was* a meteorite, and it *did* drop right into me sewage!"

"Nigel – I am prepared to fully accept this part of your account."

"Oh. Well, I'm glad about that because..."

"What I am *not* prepared to believe, however, is your statement that you heard the meteorite scream the word 'rhubarb' just before the moment of impact." Behind his desk, Mr Hodgson drew himself up to his full height before continuing. "Clearly your powers of observation have faded since you won your *Employee of the Month* award. As you no longer possess the qualities that are essential for the position, I regret to inform you that you are dismissed as of now."

*

Frogarty's words as she tramped across the fields towards her cottage, clutching her broken broomstick cannot be printed here. Though she was a filthy, smelly old thing at the best of times, plunging into the vat of raw sewage had been a bit too rich, even for her. As she squelched along, reflecting bitterly on the events of the day, it occurred to her that, although rhubarb had its merits, she perhaps did not love it *quite* enough to justify the trials and tribulations involved in obtaining the stuff.

"It'll be Fly Pie every time from now on," she grumbled. "Or Jellied Earwigs..."

On her arrival back at Spittleflap Cottage, Frogarty did something very unusual - Yes reader - Frogarty had a *wash*.

"Tumty tumty tum," she hummed horribly as she scrubbed her armpits.

"Fly Pie, Fly Pie, Fly Pie for tea,
Fly Pie, Fly Pie – It's the only pud for me!"

Satisfied that most, if not quite all, of the sewage had been removed from her person, she dressed hurriedly and waddled through to the larder where she knew that a huge jar of juicy bluebottles, the essential ingredient for Fly Pie, awaited her.

"Eek!" she screeched as she observed the empty vessel. *"Me flies! Someone's gone and robbed all me flies!"* And then Frogarty noticed something. On the shelf, right next to the jar, there were some footprints. Small, round, footprints.

"*Scratch!*" she wailed, almost in tears, such was her inner rage. "*Scratch! You miserable, filching feline! You've robbed me flies!*" Furiously, she stomped around the cottage, ransacking her way through the tiny, cluttered rooms, determined to exact a swift and savage revenge on her pilfering pet.

But Scratch was nowhere to be found. As soon as his mangy ears had detected the unmistakeable sound of his mistress's squelching approach through the forest, he had slipped away into the woods and was now fast asleep, high up in the bows of an old oak tree, purring contentedly as he dreamed of delicious, succulent, scrumptious Fly Pie…

Frogarty's Beastly Birthday

Gladys and her husband Frank stood shivering on the street corner. Beside them was a big, red post box.

"Are you absolutely *certain* you know what you are doing, Gladys?" Frank croaked, drawing his scarf ever more tightly around his neck against the freezing wind. "You *do* remember what happened last time, don't you?"

"I've *told* you, Frank! That was twenty-three years ago. She's *bound* to have mellowed a bit by now. Besides, don't forget what's at stake - it will all seem worthwhile when we get our hands on it…"

And yet for all of her bravado, it was not only the winter's chill that caused Gladys' hand to tremble as she dropped her letter into the post box that day…

*

"Scratch!" Frogarty bellowed, far more loudly than was necessary in the confines of her tiny cottage. "I've been thinking – You'd better get out there and check that mail box. It's me birthday today and no doubt I shall get a lot of cards again this year."

From his warm spot on the hearth rug, Scratch let out a miserable sigh. Frogarty *never, ever* received any cards on her birthday, first and foremost because she did not have any friends. In fact, the horrid old witch never received any post at all, not even bills. After all, there was no electricity in her isolated cottage, no gas, not even any running water. In spite of the above, each year, around the time of her birthday, she would force her long-suffering pet to venture to the rusty old mailbox at the edge of the wood in order to check it for cards.

"Yes," she continued. "I expect I shall be *inundated* with cards again this year…"

And so, as the winter sun slowly climbed across the sky that January morning, Scratch's scrawny frame could be observed slinking its way through the silent wood, his cold little paws leaving tiny prints in the snow as he went. As the trees began to thin, the rusted mailbox came into view. At first glance, it looked exactly the same as it always did, the wooden post driven into the ground at a slightly crooked angle, the legend "Frogarty Spittleflap," painted crudely on its tarnished surface. Yet this year, a sixth sense told him that something had changed. Sure enough, the thick shroud of cobwebs that normally covered the mailbox door had recently been disturbed. Warily, as though stalking a bird, Scratch crept forward to investigate…

Back at the cottage, Frogarty was busy dusting.

"*Dusting?*" I hear you cry. *"Surely a filthy old witch wouldn't bother to clean her house?"* In this instance, reader, your scepticism is well placed. In Frogarty's twisted mind, the term 'dusting' referred to the process of *adding*, rather than removing dust from her windows and furniture. Indeed, nothing upset her more than the sight of a clean mantelpiece or a shiny sink; thus, at the beginning of each week, she would take a bag of dust which she had pilfered from people's dustbins in Lower Bottomton, the nearest town, and sprinkle it liberally about the cottage until everything had a nice, thick coating.

Meanwhile, Scratch approached the cottage apprehensively. Even worse than the cold trek through the wood to the mailbox each year, was Frogarty's reaction when he returned empty handed. Or empty *pawed*, if you prefer. Usually she would begin by wailing that nobody loved her. She would then work herself up into a rage, using vulgar words that should never be used, *especially* by little old ladies, the performance climaxing with a random hurling of household objects hither and thither. Though she was only short in stature, Frogarty had the physique of a Russian shot-putter, making the tiny cottage a very dangerous place to be when she was in full flow. But this year, Scratch hoped, things would be different; this year, for the first time ever, there had been an envelope in the mailbox.

"What did I tell you, eh?" Frogarty grinned hideously as she held it up to the light. "I wonder who it's from."

Scratch quivered with trepidation.

"Perhaps it's from the Queen. Or Joan Collins. Or David Beckham. Yes – I expect it'll be from David. He usually sends me a card. Let's open it and see, shall we?"

Scratch cowered behind the sofa as Frogarty plonked her fat little bottom down in her rocking chair and, chewing her whiskery upper lip in concentration, began to read. Several minutes passed in silence. Frogarty was *not* a particularly good reader.

"It's from me sister, Gladys," she croaked, finally. "She wants me to go to tea. Tonight." Although she was pleased to receive such an invitation, Frogarty's joy was mingled with a degree of puzzlement; she, herself, had not forgotten the unfortunate incident that had occurred the last time she had visited her sister and was somewhat surprised to receive a further invitation. *Could it be that after all these years, Gladys and her husband, Frank, had found it in their hearts to forgive her?* "Scratch! Go through to the bathroom and fetch me makeup set! Hurry up – she wants us there for six!"

*

"Go and answer it then!" Gladys hissed at her husband when the doorbell sounded.

"You answer it! She's your blinking sister!"

"I *won't* tell you again, Frank!"

As he approached the door, Frank's nerve faltered. Through the frosted glass of the porch, he could discern the dull outline of a small, hunched figure. Recalling Frogarty's previous visit, a wave of nausea swept over him, causing his hand to tremble as he reached for the latch.

"Hullo Frank!" she squawked cheerfully as he opened the door. "I've come for me tea! Is Gladys in?"

Frank gawped in speechless horror. The last time he had seen Frogarty, she had been so gruesome that it had physically hurt his eyes to behold her. Alas, the twenty-three year interlude since then had served only to *worsen* her appearance, if that were indeed possible. Her makeup, though liberally administered, did nothing to ease her frightful demeanour. Frogarty, you see, did not possess a mirror, having cracked the one in her bedroom with her ghastly reflection the first time she had looked into it. Consequently, her bright-red lipstick and purple eye-shadow, blindly applied, lent her the resemblance of a diabolical clown, a grinning gargoyle from the pits of hell.

"Y… Y… Yes," Frank stammered. "She… She's just through in the kitchen. P… Please - Come in."

Although Gladys was Frogarty's sister, she was not a witch. When she had first emerged into the world, her mother (who *was* a witch) had been horrified to discover that she had given birth to a normal, attractive baby. Unable to comprehend how this could have happened (especially since her first child, Frogarty, was such a splendidly hideous specimen) it occurred to Gangarena (for that was her name) that, if the Council of Witches ever got wind of this, she would be a laughing stock! Thus she had hastily wrapped the infant in a shawl, flown to the nearest town in the dead of night on her broomstick and deposited Gladys on the steps of the orphanage. It was only after the abandoned child had grown into an adult and announced her engagement to a wealthy businessman that Gangarena decided that it might be worth re-establishing contact with her long-lost daughter.

CRASH! At the sight of her sister, Gladys had dropped the plate of nibbles she was carrying onto the tiled kitchen floor.

"Frogarty!" she exclaimed, struggling to regain her composure. "How *nice* to see you. We're *so* glad you could come, aren't we Frank?" She glared at her embattled husband who was still goggling in horror at their visitor.

"Aren't we Frank?" Gladys repeated, her voice lowering to a threatening hiss.

"Yes Frogarty," her husband gibbered. "We're simply delighted..." A sharp jab in the ribs from Gladys prompted him to continue. "Oh yes... Er... Can I get you an *aperitif*?"

"Eh?" Frogarty glowered. "A parrot's *what?* Why would I want a *parrot*? I've come 'ere for me tea. At least that's what it said on the invitation..."

"I'm sorry," Frank cringed. "I meant to ask you whether you would like something to drink before we sit down for our tea."

"Why didn't you then, instead of speaking all that nonsense about parrots? Yes – I shall have some juice."

"Juice? I think we have some orange or apple..."

"Slug."

"Pardon?"

"Slug juice will be fine. I'm not a fussy person."

Frank turned to his wife in dismay, only to discover that she had disappeared into the dining room.

"I... I think we've run out, he stammered."

“Don’t worry - I’ve brought me own,” Frogarty cackled. Rummaging beneath the folds of her shawl, she triumphantly produced a small, green bottle and, after removing the cork stopper, took a deep swig of the contents. “Would you like a drop?” she grimaced, grey slime dribbling down her pointed chin as she proffered the bottle towards her horrified host.

Speechless with revulsion, his face white as a ghost, Frank tottered from the room in search of his wife.

*

“Did you enjoy that?” Gladys forced a smile as she studied her repulsive relative across the dining table.

“Oh yes,” Frogarty burped. “Though some of it was a bit crunchy. Me teeth aren’t what they used to be, you know.”

Realizing that there was little point in trying to explain to her sister that she was not meant to have eaten the bones on her pork chop, Gladys decided that it was time to steer the conversation towards more important matters. Her motive for inviting Frogarty to tea was not one of kindness; indeed, given the choice, Gladys and Frank would have preferred to live out the rest of their lives avoiding any further contact with their unpleasant relation. But she had something that they wanted, that they needed desperately, hence their brave decision to send the invitation.

"So, what have you been up to, Frogarty?" Gladys enquired, casting a devious sideways glance at her husband.

"Eh? Nothing much. Just the usual stuff… You know – making potions, casting spells, flying about the place on me broomstick…"

"And do you still have a cat?"

"Scratch? Yes – He's here."

"Here?"

"Yes - He's just out in the garden."

"In *our* garden?" Gladys sounded concerned. "I do hope he won't frighten the birds away."

"Oh no. He won't frighten 'em away." Frogarty chuckled strangely. "You needn't worry about *that*."

Her sister's words struck Gladys as being somewhat odd, but she decided not to pursue the matter. The sooner that the important business with Frogarty could be concluded, the sooner they would be rid of her.

"Anyway," she ventured. "We're glad that you are ok, because *we've* been having a *terrible* time, haven't we, Frank?"

"Oh yes. A *terrible* time," her husband blurted, prompted by a sharp kick from his wife beneath the table.

"It's Frank's business, you see," Gladys continued doggedly.

"Eh?" Frogarty grunted. She was by now growing very bored with the conversation and was anxious to move on to dessert.

"Frank's frozen pea business. The company's fallen on hard times - I blame it on all these blasted TV chefs going on all the time about using fresh ingredients. Frozen pea sales have plummeted these last few years, haven't they Frank?"

"Er… Yes Gladys. Plummeted."

Frogarty sighed, making it clear to her hosts that she was not remotely interested in frozen pea sales, healthy or otherwise.

"But the banks are calling in their debts," Gladys was growing ever more anxious, dismayed at her sister's lack of concern. "If the firm goes bust, we could lose our home!"

"Well you can't come and live with me," Frogarty began to rise from her seat. "There's only one bedroom in me cottage and Scratch doesn't take kindly to strangers…"

"Oh no," Gladys cut in hastily, horrified at the very mention of moving in with her sister. "Of course, we wouldn't *dream* of imposing on your kind hospitality."

"Good."

"But we were wondering if you might be able to help in some other way…"

"Help?" Frogarty had never helped anyone before and was not even quite sure of the meaning of the word.

"Yes."

"Some other way?"

Taking this as her cue, Gladys launched into her pre-prepared speech with impassioned gusto.

"You see, I was down at the library…"

"Library?" Frogarty had never been in a library.

"Yes," Gladys continued breathlessly. "I was down at the library delving into our family tree."

"Oh?" Frogarty shuffled awkwardly on her plump posterior, knowing full well that her family tree was a roll call of some of the most evil characters ever to walk the earth and that delving into it was therefore inadvisable.

"Yes, and some of the things I discovered were quite fascinating."

"Oh?"

Gladys leaned across the table, bringing her face as close as she could bear to that of her gruesome sister.

"Tell me this, Frogarty. *Have you, by any chance, ever heard of our Great, Great, Great Aunt Frumpanella?"*

Frogarty started visibly, almost toppling from her dining chair.

"No," she replied after a few seconds. "I've never 'eard of her."

"That's such a pity, isn't it, Frank?"

"Eh? Oh yes – It's such a pity."

"You see, Frogarty, in this book I was reading in the library, there was a whole chapter about her."

"Oh?"

Gladys went on to explain that, according to local legend, Frumpanella had been a very beautiful witch who had lived over two hundred years ago. She had allegedly acquired her vast fortune through foul means, including a jewel known as the *Star of Al Najaf,* one of the largest diamonds ever to have been mined, which she had stolen from an Arabian Prince who had succumbed to her dubious charms.

"And when she died," Gladys continued determinedly, "it is believed that she left all of her wealth to her niece, Gangarena, *our mother."*

"Oh, she did, did she?" Frogarty fidgeted. "Well it's the first I've ever heard of it!"

But Gladys was in full flow and was not prepared to let the matter drop.

"Yet the book does not reveal anything about what happened to the money when our mother died," she persisted.

"Oh well – I expect she must have spent it."

"Well Frank and I don't believe she did."

"Oh?"

"No, Frogarty. Frank and I believe that she would have left it to her daughters, to you and me. Half each."

"Poppycock! I don't know what you're talking about. Now are we going to have some pudding or what?"

"*Please* Frogarty!" Gladys' voice now took on a pleading tone. "If you have all of Frumpella's fortune, *surely* you can see that it ought to be shared with *me*. It's only fair."

"*Fair?*" Frogarty did not believe in fairness. Foulness was her thing.

"Yes. Can't you see? It's what Mother would have wanted!"

Now it was Frogarty's turn to rise to her feet. As she was only roughly half the height of her sister, she cut a less than imposing figure.

"Like I just said, I've *no idea* what you're talking about. Now – if you don't mind, I thought that Scratch and me would take care of the pudding."

"But…"

"Scratch!" Frogarty roared through the open kitchen window. *"Come on! Bring in them ingredients so we can get the pudding on the go."*

There was a brief pause, followed by a persistent clawing sound at the back door.

"That'll be 'im now. I'll just let 'im in."

Frank and Gladys could only gape in horror as the door opened wide and Scratch crossed the threshold, dragging a bulging cloth sack in his wake. The sack, they noticed, appeared to be filled with something that was alive.

"Did you manage to get enough of 'em?" Frogarty enquired anxiously.

Scratch nodded his mangy head and, in doing so, lost his grip on the mouth of the sack which had been clenched between his teeth. What followed is what is often referred to as *pandemonium.* It had been Frogarty's intention to delight her hosts with one of her favourite signature dishes: blackbird pie. As we all know from the nursery rhyme, a blackbird pie ideally contains *"four and twenty black birds,"* and it was this ingredient that Scratch had been diligently collecting in and around the garden whilst his owner had been chatting with their hosts.

Have you ever had twenty-four medium-sized, garden birds flying frantically around your kitchen? If you ever happen to bump into them, Frank and Gladys will no doubt confirm that it is not something to be recommended under any circumstances, especially if, like Gladys, you suffer from ornithophobia. Ornithophobia, you see, is word which means *a fear of birds*. Even the sight of a solitary mallard in her local park was enough to make Gladys nervous; thus it is not difficult to imagine the impact of twenty-four black birds fluttering around her head in a confined space. After a bout of unrestrained shrieking, the poor woman collapsed in a fit of hysterics before passing out altogether.

Frogarty shook her head in bemusement at the sight of Frank dragging his wife's inert form from the kitchen to the relative safety of the upstairs bedroom.

"I wonder what's up with her?" she mused, rubbing her long, pimply chin. "Never mind - I shall get on with the pie anyway. Perhaps it'll make her feel better. Now – where's the oven?"

As we mentioned earlier in the story, due to the remote location of her cottage, Frogarty did not have any experience of using gas. Indeed, all of her cooking to date had been done in a cauldron over an open fire. Thus, when she began to twiddle with the knobs on her sister's gas oven, she had no way of knowing that the resultant *hissing* sound, together with a distinctive smell, was that of escaping gas which quickly began to fill the kitchen.

"Scratch!" she barked. "What's that hissing noise? What's that smell? What have I told you about trumping indoors?"

Scratch did not reply. Sensing that something catastrophic was about to happen, he had already retreated back outside into the garden.

Meanwhile, Frogarty was growing increasingly frustrated at her lack of progress in the kitchen.

"I can't get this flippin' thing to work!" she crowed at nobody in particular. By now the room was so full of gas that it made even Frogarty feel strange. "I'll just have to make a little fire on the floor and cook me blackbirds in a pot just like I do at home in me cauldron. Now where does Gladys keep her matches…"

*

The sound of Frank and Gladys' house exploding could be heard in three adjoining counties. Although several fire engines arrived quickly at the scene, there was nothing they could do to salvage the building, or indeed any of Frank and Gladys' possessions. Everything they owned, everything they had ever possessed was utterly destroyed in the inferno.

Miraculously, Frank and Gladys survived; they had been in the upstairs bathroom when the explosion occurred, Frank trying to revive his wife with cold water from the sink. When the enormous *BANG* had rocked the house, they had fallen on top of one another into the bathtub, the porcelain sides acting as a shield from the worst of the blast.

Although she was in the kitchen, and therefore right at the epicentre of the explosion, Frogarty also survived. How this could be has never been adequately explained, however, we can only conclude that witches must made of sterner stuff than we mere mortals are thus not easily disposed of.

Scratch, for his part, escaped with a mere singing of the fur, strategically positioned as he was out in the garden. People say that cats have nine lives; in his dealings with Frogarty, Scratch had, in all probability used these up several times over, but he nevertheless lived to fight another day on this occasion.

*

"Well – I shan't be visiting Frank and Gladys again in a hurry!" Frogarty grumbled as she reached for her spell book. "Did you *see* the way they looked at us as they were being stretchered into that ambulance? Didn't even bother to say cheerio! What a way to treat guests!"

Scratch merely yawned, shivering slightly as a freezing wind blew underneath the crooked cottage door.

"Tsk!" Frogarty tutted as the draught turned over the pages of her spell book. "Now I've lost me page again! Scratch – get yourself down to the cellar and fetch me that paperweight. You know the one I mean? That big shiny one…"

Seconds later, Scratch was back, clutching in his teeth *The Star of Al Najaf,* the priceless diamond that Frogarty's mother had left to her many, many years ago.

*

Is there a moral to this tale? Does it teach us that material greed and lust for money can only bring misery? Personally, I don't think so - In *my* opinion, the most important lesson we can learn from the story is that, no matter what the circumstances may be, one should *never, ever* invite Frogarty round to one's house for tea…

Frogarty's Horrible Hobby.

"I'm fed up, Scratch!" Frogarty exclaimed, rising suddenly from her rickety rocking chair.

Scratch did not reply; being a cat, he was unable to do so. Instead, he merely yawned, deftly removing a flea from behind his left ear using his back leg.

"And *you're* no company!" his mistress continued irritably. "All you ever do is mooch about the place all day waiting to be fed."

Scratch sighed. *What, exactly, did the old twit expect him to do? He was a cat, for goodness sake! He could hardly assist with the housework, nor could he entertain her with witty anecdotes. Indeed, he could only really do what cats are best at - mooching around the house all day waiting to be fed...*

"Well – I've had enough!" Frogarty was now reaching for her pointy hat and shawl. "I'm going into town. I've decided I'm going to find myself a hobby." And with these chilling words, she waddled out of the sitting room, slamming the door behind her.

Though he was relieved to see the back of his bad-tempered owner, Scratch remained ill-at-ease as he lounged in front of the dying embers of the fire. Every six months or so, Frogarty would announce her intention to take up a hobby, and every single time, without exception, it would end in some form of unspeakable tragedy. Her last "hobby" had been stamp collecting; by the time she finally abandoned it, eleven innocent people had been hospitalised, several traditional red post boxes had been destroyed, and the Royal Mail sorting office in Lower Bottomton had been burned to the ground. The poor puss could only hope that whatever Frogarty's latest hobby turned out to be, it would not require any involvement on his part.

*

It was a pensive and somewhat nervous Frogarty that approached the outskirts of Lower Bottomton that morning. Although she was determined to take up a hobby, she did not, at this stage, have even the vaguest idea as to what *species* of hobby it would be. She did, however, know that there existed a noticeboard in the newsagent's shop window on which was there was pinned a list of all the evening classes and activities currently being held at the Community Centre. *Surely there would be something suitable for a mean and tubby little witch on there…*

"Ah yes," she gurgled as she stood on her tiptoes, peering up at the list. "That sounds like it'll be *just* the thing for me. And it starts at seven o'clock tonight! Wait 'til I tell Scratch!"

*

Mrs Carlita Latino had been running the Lower Bottomton salsa dancing class every Tuesday night for the past seven years. Carlita Latino was not her real name; her *real* name was Mavis Blathersop. When the original advertisements failed to attract students to the classes, however, it had occurred to her that her birth name arguably lacked the sense of glamour required for the role of a salsa dancing instructor, and so she had changed it. Sure enough, new recruits flooded through the door the very next week and, at nineteen pupils, the class was now *almost* operating at full capacity, with room for just one addition before fire regulations would be breached.

If truth be told, Carlita (to avoid confusion, we shall use her stage name henceforth) was not a very good dance teacher; she had no qualifications of any kind, was slightly overweight due to a love of pizza and chocolate, and was handicapped by a decidedly suspect sense of rhythm. She *had,* on the other hand, seen every episode ever broadcast of *Strictly Come Dancing* on the TV (usually whilst eating pizza and chocolate) and believed that this provided all the knowledge she would need to teach the class. Besides, there was good money to be made, and Carlita needed every penny she could get to pay for more pizza and chocolate.

As seven o'clock approached, the class members began to arrive, Carlita beaming at each in turn through her fake suntan. As always, Brenda, the supervisor from the Costalot supermarket was the first to turn up, closely followed by Mr Fetorworth from the sewage works, accompanied by his wife, Stacey.

"Now then everybody!" Carlita chimed as soon as everyone was assembled. "If you'd all like to get into your positions, we'll get started right away. We'll begin with a bit of a warm up and then I'm going to teach you *two* new steps!"

With these words, she trudged over to the CD player and was about to press play when the door at the back of the room creaked open.

"I've come to do some dancing," croaked a gruff voice.

You guessed it, folks – Frogarty had arrived to embark on her new hobby: salsa dancing.

Carlita froze. Although her view of the newcomer was somewhat obscured by the rows of eager pupils in the hall, she *had* caught a tiny glimpse of Frogarty and this was enough to confirm that here was a most unsuitable candidate.

Despite her genuine enthusiasm, Frogarty had, as a witch living deep in the woods without a television set, been unsure as to how one should dress when attending a salsa class. After much deliberation, she had decided that something exotic was called for and, having consulted her spell book, had conjured up a Hawaiian-style grass skirt with matching coconut-shell bra, a look which contrasted sharply with the plain tracksuits and t-shirts worn by the other pupils. Worse still, both the skirt *and* the bra were of a size that was wholly inadequate to cover the heaving contours of Frogarty's flabby figure. In the interests of common decency I will refrain from describing in *too* much more detail the grim spectacle that confronted Carlita that evening but will simply declare that Frogarty looked *ghastly. Frightful* would be another suitable descriptive word, as would *appalling, repulsive* or *gruesome*. Try and picture Frogarty in your mind and see if *you* can think of any more...

"I've come to do some dancing," the witch repeated, pushing her way rudely through the shocked ensemble towards the front row.

"I... I'm terribly sorry," Carlita stammered "but the class is over-subscribed."

"No it isn't. It says on that poster out there that there's a place left."

Carlita's world swam before her eyes. *Why, oh why, had she written that on the poster?*

"I'm ready when you are," Frogarty growled, taking up a commanding position right in the middle of the front row in between Mr and Mrs Fetorworth.

Gulping with nausea, Carlita fought to regain her composure. Although Frogarty was only small in stature, there was something compelling, indeed terrifying, about her that rendered most ordinary people powerless to resist her will. To her utter horror, the instructor realized that she had no choice but to continue the lesson *with* Frogarty present.

"OK," she gurgled. "We... We'll forget about the warm-up today and get straight onto teaching you those new moves I was telling you about."

Still numbed with shock at the sight of Frogarty, the other pupils simply stood rooted to the spot in horrified silence, awaiting instruction.

"Now the first move is called the *Hook Turn.* Now, what you have to do is simply place the right foot behind the left foot and turn..."

"Hang on a minute!" Frogarty exclaimed. "This grass skirt is chafing me bum something terrible..."

"P... Please Mrs... Mrs?"

"Spittleflap. Frogarty Spittleflap's the name!"

"Please Mrs Spittleflap. As you're a new starter, perhaps you'd just like to sit and watch the others to begin with. How about..."

"No!" Frogarty barked. "I've not come 'ere to mess about. I've come here to do me dancing. Now what's all that you were saying about a hook?"

"W... Well, yes. I thought we'd begin with that because..."

But Frogarty wasn't listening. Eager to impress her new teacher, she had already decided that she would proceed alone, without any need for further guidance. *Besides, she already knew what a hook was; it was a type of powerful punch used in boxing, another of her previous hobbies that had ended in tragedy.* Frogarty couldn't quite work out what punching someone had to do with salsa dancing, but if that was what the teacher wanted, then so be it...

WHAM!

A scream went up from Mrs Fetorworth as her husband was felled by a sickeningly powerful blow from the diminutive witch. As the stricken man was carried away to the toilets to be revived by his appalled fellow pupils, Frogarty turned to her teacher, expecting to receive some form of praise for her neat handiwork.

Though badly shaken, Carlita felt a sudden rush of anger welling up inside her; *she had worked very hard to set up this salsa class and was NOT going to stand by and see it ruined by this foul little woman!*

"Frogarty!" she cried with as much authority as she could muster. "I simply *cannot* allow that kind of behaviour in my class. I'm afraid..."

"I was only doing what you said," the witch retorted defiantly, aghast at her instructor's lack of appreciation for what had, in her opinion, been an *excellent* hook. "You told me to do a hook, so I did a hook!"

Her protests went unheeded as Carlita, speechless with frustration, marched off to the toilets to check on poor Mr Fetorworth. After some minutes, they emerged arm-in-arm and re-joined the group, Frogarty noting with a vague sense of satisfaction that the unfortunate man had a large wad of tissue paper stuffed up his left nostril.

"The next step I'm going to teach you," the beleaguered teacher continued "is a wonderful turn that is known in salsa circles as *the break*." She did not notice the ominous glint that flickered into little witch's evil eyes...

"Gaaaaaaaargh!" Mr Fetorworth wailed as his right shin-bone was broken in two by a flying karate kick.

"Howzat!" Frogarty cried triumphantly, extremely proud of her effort, given the fact that it was over ten years since she had been forced to abandon karate as a hobby. Mrs Fetorworth, unable to take any more, collapsed into a swoon beside her husband on the floor.

A cry of horror went up among the rest of pupils and they stampeded as one towards the emergency exit, stumbling and trampling over one another as they went. For Carlita, the penny finally dropped; the situation had deteriorated to a degree which was beyond her modest capabilities. *Enough was enough: she would dial 999.*

"Hello," the operator's calm tones filtered down the line. "Which service do you require?"

"Ambulance!" Carlita wailed, glancing down at Mr Fetorworth's writhing, agonised form. "At the Community Centre. Please hurry!" She was about to hang up the telephone when she noticed Frogarty, patiently waiting for the lesson to resume, apparently oblivious to the chaos around her. "And you'd better send the police," Carlita added. "And tell them to wear riot gear. And bring the dogs. No – On second thoughts, forget the dogs - Bring the *army!*"

Frogarty was beginning to get more than a little fed up with this whole salsa dancing business. After all, she'd been here for almost half-an-hour and had not danced a single step.

"What we need is a bit of music," she grumbled. Deciding to take matters into her own hands, she waddled over to the CD player. Whilst her instinct told her that this strange object was capable of producing music, Frogarty had never seen a CD player before and thus had no idea how to operate one. After a brief fiddle with the buttons on the front had failed to produce the desired results, she produced her wand from somewhere beneath her grass skirt.

"Zaracabong!" she roared, pointing it at the machine. There was a *fizz,* followed by a *flash* before a lightning bolt shot from the end of the wand, setting the machine ablaze. Within seconds,

the rising flames reached the curtains in the adjacent window and the room quickly began to fill with black smoke.

"And you might as well send the fire brigade as well, please," Carlita sobbed before replacing the telephone handset.

The sound of multiple sirens approaching led Frogarty to the reluctant conclusion that perhaps salsa dancing was not for her. Like a panther, albeit a fat and out-of-condition specimen, she slipped away into the shadows of the night.

*

The following morning there was an unusual air of calmness around Spittleflap Cottage.

"Impossible!" I hear you cry. *"Nothing is ever calm when Frogarty is around!"*

Well, reader, as previously stated, everything *was* calm in Spittleflap Cottage that morning for the simple reason that Frogarty had found a new hobby, something far less perilous than salsa dancing...

"But we must not forget what happened when she took up stamp collecting!" you protest.

There, reader, you have a good point! However this latest hobby was something which was even less strenuous than stamp collecting. Yes reader, Frogarty had taken up knitting...

"Scratch!" she shrieked, placing her needles down on the floor beside her rocking chair. "I've finished another. Come through 'ere and see what you think."

Reluctantly, Scratch abandoned the decomposing rat he had discovered underneath the kitchen sink and sloped through to the living room. He had been forced to inspect his mistress's knitting output six times already this morning and was getting rather fed up, as each item was virtually identical to the last. *Why couldn't she make something useful like a nice warm blanket to go in his draughty old basket?*

"Here we are," Frogarty cackled, proudly holding aloft the fruit of her labour "Another *beautiful* cobweb for the ceiling!"

Frogarty's Frightful Halloween

Snuggled in her filthy little bed, Frogarty was awoken by a faint mewing sound which filtered beneath the bedroom door.

"Scratch?" she crowed, blinking open one wicked eye. "Is that you?"

"Meow," Scratch replied, limited as he was by his feline vocabulary.

"Well you can go away! You know what date it is, don't you?"

"Meow," the cat persisted doggedly, if cats *can* do things doggedly. Scratch did not know what the date was; all he knew was that his stomach was rumbling and that he wanted his breakfast.

"Have you forgotten what happened last Halloween? I've *told* you – This year, I'm staying here safe and sound in me lovely warm bed until it's all over!"

If you or I, reader, were ever to examine Frogarty's bed, we would doubtlessly be appalled by what we would discover therein; through her entire life (and she was over a hundred years old) she had *never, ever* changed the sheets! *Not even once!* Now that you are aware of the facts, you will not be surprised to learn that it was riddled with lice, cockroaches and many other unpleasant species as yet to be identified in scientific circles.

Despite this, Frogarty *loved* her bed; it was the one place where she felt safe from the worries of the world and she had learned to embrace, rather than exterminate any uninvited visitors. The lice, therefore, had been individually christened with her favourite girls' and boys' names and she would often say goodnight to Charlotte, David, Georgina, Barry, Andrew, Britney and the rest before she nodded off to sleep. Towards the bottom end of the mattress, where Frogarty rested her stinky feet, a toxic fungus flourished. Over the course of many, many years, this fungus had evolved to a point where it was possible to hold a rational conversation with it; indeed, Frogarty was of the opinion that her fungus offered far more stimulating company than Scratch during the long winter nights.

"Meow."

"Alright!" Frogarty cried, springing from beneath the sheets. "I'll come and get you some breakfast, but then I'm going straight back to me bed until the morning!"

*

Scratch licked his lips contentedly and curled up in his favourite spot in front of the hearth. Last night's fire had almost died out, but there was still a whisper of warmth emanating from the ashes in the grate. He had never tasted cat food as such, accustomed as he was to surviving on the leftovers from Frogarty's foul cuisine; last night, she had dined on woodlouse casserole (as it was a Tuesday) and the cold remnants of this had proven to be a tasty and satisfying breakfast.

As promised, his mistress had fed him and then returned to her bed. Given that Frogarty was not what anyone would call a *pleasant* companion and that her very presence in the same room generally increased the risk of him losing yet another of his nine lives, Scratch was more than content with this arrangement.

*

As the afternoon sunshine faded into dusk, however, Frogarty grew increasingly restless and hopped out of bed in order to peek through the curtains.

"I'll *bet* they turn up any minute now," she grunted miserably. She had not been back in her bed for more than a few seconds when, from the vicinity of the garden gate there came a low, mournful groan. Then another. Then another.

With a cry of anguish, Frogarty rushed back over to the window to investigate; *Yes – she had been right; the night had barely even begun and already the zombies had arrived...*

Every year on Halloween night, as soon darkness fell, the bodies of those who had lost their lives in the wood that surrounded the little cottage would rise from their graves and wander about the place moaning plaintively and engaging in various other forms of anti-social behaviour. They had all died in different historical times, and often were still clad in the costumes of their era, not that this was of any interest to Frogarty.

"You lot are a damned *pest!* Don't you *dare* come in here" she shrieked, leaning out of her window and shaking her knobbly fist at the rotting carcass of an eighteenth-century highwayman who was busy fiddling with the latch on the garden gate. Moments later, he was joined by a decomposing Victorian lady, still sporting the tattered remains of an elegant summer dress. But it was the sight of a corpse from the nineteen eighties, clad in a shell-suit and fluorescent trainers, infiltrating her vegetable patch which spurred Frogarty into violent action. Although the vegetable patch at Spittleflap Cottage was little more than an unkempt jungle of brambles and weeds, these brambles and weeds often came in useful as ingredients in her foul spells and she was damned if she was going to tolerate a bunch of zombies wandering about all over them...

Bustling down the creaky stairs of the cottage, cursing freely as she went, the repellent old hag snatched up her broomstick and strode menacingly out through the front door. Wielding it like a light sabre, she swished and slashed at the invading zombies with remarkable agility for a lady of more than one hundred years' vintage. In spite of her brave efforts, however, it quickly became clear that she was fighting a losing battle; barely had she driven the Victorian lady away from the fence when she espied the chap in the shell-suit trampling on her precious brambles. By the time she had driven *him* back, the highwayman had mastered the mechanics of the gate-latch and was strolling down the garden path as though he owned the place. Worse still, even *more* zombies were now emerging from the trees, all seemingly intent on invading the little cottage.

Recognising the need for a tactical withdrawal, Frogarty took a final swipe at the highwayman with her broom before turning on her heels and retreating to the relative safety of Spittleflap Cottage.

"*Flipping zombies*!" she snarled as she slammed the door shut, turning the key in the lock.

From his position behind the coal scuttle, Scratch cowered, watching his mistress nervously as she reached for her spell book. For what seemed like an eternity, she scoured the dusty pages of the huge, ancient volume, the moans of the undead in the garden growing ever louder and more insistent all the while.

"*Aha*!" Frogarty cried finally, just as a gruesome, rotting face pressed itself against the kitchen window. "This'll show 'em!"

In selecting an appropriate spell, Frogarty had faced a great dilemma; whilst *everyone* knows that the way to deal with an undead horde is simply to bring the individuals back to life, bringing things back to life is technically classified as *good* magic, a field of sorcery which is strictly forbidden to any self-respecting wicked witch. For this reason, Frogarty had been forced to settle for a spell which, though far from ideal, would at least make the zombie threat a little easier to contain.

Flinging open the front door of the cottage, she sallied forth into the garden and, from the vantage point of a rotten tree stump, cleared her throat horribly before issuing the following incantation:

"EYE OF NEWT,
AND LIZARD'S BUM,
ZOMBIE **SLUGS**,
YOU SHALL BECOME!"

There was a flash and a hiss, followed by a sound not unlike that made by a wildebeest breaking wind and then everything fell silent.

“Ha!” Frogarty chuckled. “I *knew* that would do the trick...”

Having obtained an empty jam jar from her larder, it was the simplest of tasks for her to waddle around the garden and gather up the zombie slugs; even in mollusc form, they posed a potential threat to her precious weeds and besides, she knew of a couple of good spells in which zombie slugs were a key ingredient.

“Now then, Scratch,” she growled triumphantly, carefully depositing the jam jar in her larder “I’ve sorted out them troublesome zombies so I’m off up to me bed. And I *don’t* want to be disturbed again ‘til the morning.”

“Meow.”

*

In the dark skies above the wood in which Frogarty’s little cottage stood, a huge black raven circled, its cold, green eyes searching amidst the treetops for any sign of the tiny dwelling.

Fast asleep in her bed, Frogarty did not stir when the great bird alighted on the cottage roof, nor did she awaken when it dropped something down the chimney.

Scratch, however, in his position in front of the hearth, almost jumped out of his skin when the mysterious object landed in the fire grate, showering him with soot and ashes.

“Meow!” he cried with justifiable indignation as he dived for cover behind the coal scuttle. From his hiding place, the hapless moggy watched in horror as the thing that had landed in the fireplace stirred into life. As the creature blinked its eyes open, shaking soot from its coat, Scratch was able to discern that the unexpected visitor was a rat. Usually, when confronted with such a rodent, he would attack with gusto, however, there was something about this particular specimen which unsettled him. First and foremost, it was an extremely *large* rat, roughly twice the size of that to which Scratch was accustomed. Secondly, it possessed four huge, yellow canine teeth which, in addition to being as sharp as chisels, seemed to be positively dripping with horrible diseases. In its paws, it clutched what appeared to be a small scroll of paper.

“Scratch?” Frogarty barked as she was awoken yet again by a scrabbling noise outside her bedroom door. “I’ve just about had enough of you, you flea-bitten, cloth-eared, clot!” And with these words, she leapt furiously from her bed and flung open the door.

“Eek!” she cried at the sight of the gigantic rodent. Frogarty did not like rats – she had been bitten on the end of her nose by her pet rat, Steve, when she was a child and had never quite forgotten the experience. “Scratch! It’s a rat! Come up ‘ere quick and get ‘im!”

Downstairs, Scratch cowered ever more deeply into the shadows; he had no intention of tangling with this particular rodent and was determined to maintain his policy of non-intervention for as long as he possibly could. Trembling, he tried to cover his ears with his paws in a hopeless bid to shut out the terrible sounds emanating from the upstairs landing as his mistress and the giant rodent closed in combat.

Frogarty's biggest problem was that she had left her trusty broom downstairs in the kitchen; in addition to its function as a mode of transport, she found it often came in useful as a type of clubbing weapon. Indeed, the only item readily available with which to tackle her deadly foe was the rolled-up copy of *Cosmopolitan* she had been reading before she went to sleep. Though it was far from ideal, Frogarty was able to use the celebrated fashion magazine to considerable effect, lunging and parrying with great dexterity as the raging rodent did its utmost to sink its teeth into the end of her nose (just as Steve had done many years before). Eventually, however, repeated contact with the razor-sharp fangs caused the edges of the magazine to fray and, faced with the imminent disintegration of her weapon, Frogarty was driven back into her bedroom. Sensing victory, the rat made a final, desperate lunge at his mortal foe; again the witch was able to utilise the tattered fashion rag to fend off her assailant, however the sheer violence of the attack caused her to stumble and, catching her slipper on the rug, she hit the floor with a sickening *THUMP*.

Flatulence is another word for *windy pops* and can be a terrible and embarrassing affliction for those who suffer with it. And yet, on this occasion, it was Frogarty's flatulence which proved to be her saviour. We have already alluded to the fact that she had, the previous evening, dined on woodlouse casserole, a dish notorious for its wind-inducing properties. *Who could have guessed that this would come to her rescue in her hour of need?*

"Frrrrrrrrrrrrrut!!!" Frogarty's bottom exclaimed as the impact of the fall squeezed her fat belly like a set of bellows, forcing out the toxic gasses which had been fermenting therein from her plump posterior.

The rat stopped dead in its tracks. It blinked and narrowed its evil eyes before making the greatest mistake of its career thus far; you guessed it, reader... it sniffed the air...

You would be forgiven for thinking that a lifetime of living in sewers and grovelling around garbage bins ought to have provided the rat with the relevant experience to deal with a simple bit of wind. However, the smell that escaped from Frogarty's rear end that cold October evening was much more than a "simple bit of wind." Although no words could ever do justice to the heady aroma that rapidly filled the bedroom, I believe it to be my duty as narrator of the tale to at least give it a go...

Try to imagine the stench given off by a decomposing badger lying dead at the side of the road, then combine this with a hefty dose of rotten eggs, a whiff of dog food and the aroma of a labourer's armpit, and you will be getting close to the mark. Add a sniff of mackerel paste and you are almost there...

The best we can say for the poor, unsuspecting rat, was that it did not suffer a long, agonising demise; indeed, the aroma was so overpowering that the poor creature's heart simply stopped, causing it to drop dead in an instant.

"Ha ha!" Frogarty crowed triumphantly as she used her copy of *Cosmopolitan* to prod her vanquished enemy down the staircase. "That'll teach you! Now, once and for all, I'm off to me bed!" But as she turned back towards the bedroom, she spotted the little scroll which the rat had dropped in the heat of combat.

"Drat!" she cursed as, suspecting the worst, she stooped to gather up the document. Its contents were as follows:

"*Dear Frogarty,*

I am writing to remind you that, what with tonight being Halloween and all that, you are, as a member of the Grand Council of Witches, expected to get out and about terrorising the general public as much as possible. Failure to carry out your duty (and I shall be checking!) will result in the severest of penalties (and by that, I mean DEATH). Yours sincerely, Doreen Beresford, Queen of Witches."

"Damn and flip!" Frogarty cried. "Well I'm not going! I shall say I was ill... Yes... I shall say I had one of them *migraine* thingies..."

Downstairs, meanwhile, Scratch leapt up in terror as a second large, black object landed in the hearth, sending up a great cloud of ash. You guessed it – it was another monstrous rat, even bigger than the first and, just like its predecessor, it clutched a small scroll in its paws.

"Gaaaaaaah!" Frogarty wailed as she spotted her new adversary scampering up the stairs. The *Cosmopolitan* magazine was on its last legs and would not survive another skirmish. Fortunately, this particular rat seemed strangely reluctant to take up the gauntlet; perhaps he was just feeling a little below par that evening, or (and I believe this to be the more likely explanation) it may have been that his sensitive nostrils still detected a residue of Frogarty's wind lingering in the atmosphere. Whatever the reason, it simply dropped the scroll at the witch's feet and withdrew gracefully.

"Hmmf! Whatever next?" With a heavy heart, Frogarty opened the scroll to read its contents aloud:

"And don't go thinking you can get off with saying you've got a migraine like you tried to do last year. All my love, Doreen."

*

As she headed into Lower Bottomton on her trusty broomstick that night, Frogarty brooded darkly on the gross injustices of life. *So what if she was a witch? So what if Halloween was the one and only night of the year when she was expected to work?* Lost in thought, she failed to notice a telegraph pole looming through the dusk and the resulting collision left her dangling like a gruesome puppet among the telegraph wires, her broomstick plummeting to the ground below. With grim determination, Frogarty succeeded in extricating herself, dropping like a brick into a deep puddle in the road. Bruised and dripping with mud, she continued on her way, feeling as nasty as nasty can be. *If Doreen Beresford wanted her to frighten people, then frighten them she would! She would show that meddling old hag a thing or two...*

Arriving on the outskirts of town, she sighted a group of children; there must have been five or six of the little blighters, all dressed in Halloween costume.

"Ah ha! My first victims!" Frogarty cackled gleefully. Keeping to the shadows, she stalked along the high street towards the huddled group who were engrossed in an argument about the proposed route for their trick-or-treating rounds.

"It's not *fair* - *You* did Cromartie Street last year!" a spotty youth dressed as a vampire was protesting. "The people in those big houses always give you *loads* of good stuff."

"I know, Trevor, but I can't do George Street 'cos my Auntie lives there and she'll recognise me, so it's best if you and Podge..."

"Gaaaaaaaaaaaah!" Frogarty yelled, springing forth from the darkness. To her considerable chagrin, none of the children batted an eyelid, instead continuing their conversation as though nothing had happened. "Gaaaarggh!" she repeated with considerably less conviction.

"Look, will you *please* keep it down!" the spotty youth turned to her in exasperation. "We're *trying* to decide who's going where, and we can't concentrate with you making all that racket."

"Racket?" The tubby little witch was almost speechless with indignation.

"Yes – Now either shut up or go home." Spotty Trevor was the top dog amongst the kids in Lower Bottomton and was not prepared to stand for any nonsense from the vertically-challenged newcomer.

"Shut up? Go home?" Frogarty stamped her foot with rage. "But I'm a *witch*!"

"Yes, we can see that. The thing is, you're not coming trick-or-treating with us in that rubbish costume..."

"*Rubbish costume*?"

"Yes – it looks really cheap and tatty."

"*Cheap and tatty*?"

"And as for that awful mask?"

"*Awful mask*?"

"It's *so* unrealistic – even real witches aren't *that* ugly!"

Being turned into a toad was perhaps not such a bad fate for Spotty Trevor; indeed, one could say that the transformation arguably *improved* his complexion. A bully at school who was disliked by almost everyone he had ever met, including his parents, Trevor would not be missed in the slightest. Thus, by turning him into a toad, Frogarty had unwittingly performed a *good* deed, an act which would land her in serious trouble with Doreen Beresford, Queen of Witches, were she ever to hear of it.

Noting the fate of their leader, the rest of the gang fled in terror and never set foot out of their front doors on Halloween night for the rest of their days.

Frogarty, sorely wounded by Trevor's critique of her appearance, continued on her way in search of fresh victims. She waddled up one street, then down another but there was not a soul to be seen. *How the devil was she meant to terrorise folk when there was nobody around to terrorise? If the streets were deserted, there was only one thing for it; she would have to knock on some doors and frighten people in their own homes!*

The first house that she came to had a notice tacked to the door:

NO TRICK OR TREATERS!

"Hmph!" Frogarty huffed. "We'll soon see about *that*!"

And so she knocked loudly: no response. Certain that she had seen one of the curtains in an upstairs window twitch, she knocked a second time, even louder than before: still no response. Never one to give up easily, the cantankerous old hag began to pummel the door repeatedly with the end of her broomstick; for a witch, Frogarty had a rather good sense of rhythm and she soon discovered that, by alternating blows with her fist and the handle of her broom, it was possible to achieve something resembling a lively salsa beat. She was debating whether to slip into a brisk rumba when the door creaked open.

Silhouetted in the doorway was the figure of an extremely tall and heavily built man; even in the poor light, Frogarty was able to clearly discern his shaven head and bulging muscles. As her eyes gradually adjusted, she noticed that he was holding something in both hands... *A bucket... But why would a complete stranger be offering her a bucket?*

When the water made contact with Frogarty, she did not sink to the ground, hissing and fizzing, as some witches have a tendency to do; instead, she merely stood, rooted to the spot, feeling very, very wet. *That was it! She was done with Halloween once and for all! Doreen Beresford and all the other witches on the High Council could go and boil their heads are far as she was concerned.* Her mind made up, Frogarty began the long squelch home...

She had not travelled for more than a few paces, however, when she became aware of what is sometimes referred to as a "hubbub" emanating from behind the front door of another house on the opposite side of the street. Crossing the road to investigate, her ears detected the muffled sound of music playing and the buzz of many voices, laughing and having a good time. *Could this be her last chance to redeem herself?*

"Aha!" she grinned. "A *party!* If I can get in there and *completely* ruin it, Doreen will be over the moon! Why – I might even be nominated for the Wicked Witch of the Year Award! That'll show 'em..."

Bustling across the street, she rang the doorbell and waited. Seconds later, the door was opened by a young man dressed as Frankenstein's monster.

“Well *hello* there,” he beamed at the squat, soggy figure on the doorstep. “*Love* the costume! Come on in and join the fun...”

*

In her secret headquarters in the frozen wastes of the North, Doreen Beresford, Queen of Witches, sifted through her enormous pile of newspapers until she came across the *Lower Bottomton Gazette*. Every year, on the first of November, it was her practice to check the pages of dozens of newspapers from around the world for articles detailing the dastardly deeds carried out by her legions of witches over Halloween. For some time now, Lower Bottomton, which fell under Frogarty’s jurisdiction, had been a cause for great concern; there was a widely held view among the witches of the High Council that Frogarty Spittleflap had, of late, been failing to pull her weight in matters of general villainy. She was, they said, too fat, too lazy, too stupid and well past her sell-by date. This year’s Halloween, they had decided, would be her last chance to prove that she was still up to the job. It was thus with considerable interest and expectation that Doreen skimmed through Lower Bottomton’s leading publication. She did not have to skim very far before she came across the following article:

Quietest Halloween Ever in Lower Bottomton.

Last night, the residents of Lower Bottomton enjoyed the most uneventful Halloween ever in the town's history, with a record low number of reported incidents of trick-or-treating. One local boy, Trevor Cooper, was reported as missing, however, his parents have issued a heartfelt plea to both the Police and the general public NOT to bother searching too hard...

"Oh Dear," Doreen growled to herself. "Oh dear, oh dear, oh dear..."

*

Snuggled in her filthy little bed, Frogarty was awoken by a loud knocking on her front door.

"Scratch?" she crowed, blinking open one wicked eye. "Is that you?"

Scratch did not reply; he had set off to London at the crack of dawn to find his fortune, having heard that the streets were paved with gold. His only regret was that he had been unable to find a sturdy pair of boots for the trip in his mistress's wardrobe. He had not travelled far before it became painfully apparent that that Frogarty's old stilettos were but a poor substitute...

BANG, BANG, BANG went the door knocker.

"Alright!" Fograty clucked, pulling on her dressing gown and slippers. "Flipping heck! Anyone would think the world was coming to an end!"

With these fateful words, she flung open the front door of Spittleflap Cottage; there on the doorstep, its eyes filled with hungry malice, teeth dripping with poisoned drool, stood a black rat the size of a grizzly bear .

"Wait there a minute," Frogarty croaked. *She was getting too old for this palaver*... With a weary sigh of resignation, she headed indoors to get her tattered copy of *Cosmopolitan* magazine. But she was too late; the second her back was turned, the creature was upon her, sending her plump form crashing to the ground. As the rat rose on its haunches, baring its teeth for the final kill, a curious sound came from the vicinity of the tubby witch who was squashed beneath its hulking form.

"Frrrrrrrrrrrrrut!!!"

THE END

OTHER TITLES BY JAMES SUTHERLAND

NORBERT

NORBERT'S SUMMER HOLIDAY

CHRISTMAS WITH NORBERT

NORBERT TO THE RESCUE

ROGER THE FROG

THE TALE OF THE MISEROUS MIP

JIMMY BLACK AND THE CURSE OF POSEIDON

NORBERT - THE COLLECTION

Visit **www.jamessutherlandbooks.com** for more information and all the latest news!

About the Author

James Sutherland was born in Stoke-on-Trent, England, many, many, many years ago. So long ago, in fact, that he can't remember a thing about it. The son of a musician, he moved around lots as a youngster, attending schools in the Isle of Man and Spain before returning to Stoke where he lurked until the age of 18. After gaining a French degree at Bangor University, North Wales, James toiled manfully at a variety of office jobs before making a daring escape through a fire exit, hell-bent on writing silly nonsense full-time. James was a big fan of Richmal Crompton's "Just William" books as a kid and has been spotted giggling at P.G. Woodhouse and George MacDonald Fraser's "Flashman" books (to name a couple of favourites) in adulthood. In his spare time, James enjoys hunting for slugs in the garden, chatting with his gold fish and frolicking around the house in his tartan nightie.

48827618R10042

Made in the USA
Middletown, DE
28 September 2017